71 ✓

Lowe, Patricia Tracy.
　　The little horse of seven colors, and other Portuguese
folk tales. Retold by Patricia Tracy Lowe from translations from the Portuguese by Anne Marie Jauss. Illustrated by Anne Marie Jauss. New York, World Pub. Co.
₁1970₎

　　122 p.　illus.　22 cm.　$4.95

　　Twenty-seven Portuguese folktales and Portuguese versions of
stories from other European countries.

　　1. Tales, Portuguese. ₁1. Folklore—Portugal₎　ɪ. Jauss, Anne
Marie, illus.　ɪɪ. Title.

PZ8.1.L95Li　　　　　　　398.2　　　　　　76–101842
　　　　　　　　　　　　　　　　　　　　　　　　　MARC

　　　　　　　　　　　　　71 ₁4₎　　　　　　　　　AC

THE LITTLE HORSE OF SEVEN COLORS

THE LITTLE HORSE OF SEVEN COLORS

AND OTHER PORTUGUESE FOLK TALES

Retold by PATRICIA TRACY LOWE

from translations from the Portuguese by
ANNE MARIE JAUSS

Illustrated by ANNE MARIE JAUSS

THE WORLD PUBLISHING COMPANY
NEW YORK AND CLEVELAND

Published by The World Publishing Company
110 East 59th Street, New York, New York 10022
Published simultaneously in Canada by
Nelson, Foster & Scott Ltd.
Library of Congress catalog card number: 76-101842
Text copyright © 1970 by Patricia Tracy Lowe
Illustrations copyright © 1970 by Anne Marie Jauss
Printed in the United States of America.
Designed by Jack Jaget

CONTENTS

INTRODUCTION   7

NOTES   13

THE LITTLE HORSE OF SEVEN COLORS   17

BORN TO BE RICH   22

THE TEN DWARFS OF AUNT GREENWATER   27

THE VIPER AND THE FRIAR'S ROPE   30

THE PRICE OF EGGS   32

THE FOOLISH LAD AND THE FLIES   36

HOW THE WILD BOARS CAME TO BE   38

BOLA BOLA   41

THE MIRACULOUS FLUTE   44

THE SHOEMAKER   47

THE LEGEND OF THE ALMOND TREE   50

SNOW IN THE MOUNTAINS   52

THE TIPSY ROOSTER   55

NO SUPPER   58

THE PIRA GAME   62

AUNT MISERY   64

GOOD LUCK AND GREAT RICHES   67

THE STRING OF LIES   72

THE MASTER OF MAGIC AND SPELLS   75

THE TAIL OF THE CAT   81

PEDRO DE MALAS ARTES, OR CLUMSY PEDRO   84

CLARINHA   90

THE LISTENING KING   95

THE MONKEY'S POMEGRANATE   97

THE OWL AND THE WOLF   103

THE COW MAIDEN   106

THE COCKROACH AND THE MOUSE   114

INTRODUCTION

Everywhere in the world people tell stories to each other. The Portuguese are no exception. Down through the centuries the storyteller has enthralled his listeners with tales of princesses and giants, dragons and the Devil, animals, sorcerers, and witches. Portugal is very rich in her heritage of folk tales. Sometimes these stories were sung. Sometimes they were in the form of a game. But most of them were told by one person to another, and as time went on they changed little by little so that the same story heard by a listener differed from that heard by his grandmother. A few of them were written down and preserved unchanged.

Many of the folk tales of Portugal are versions of those known and loved in other European countries: *Cinderella, Hansel and Gretel, Snow White and Rose Red, Thumbling,* and *The Valiant Little Tailor.* But Portugal also has stories found only in that country, that describe the Portuguese way of life, the people's own customs and beliefs, their religion, their behavior, all the things they feel important.

Folk tales often give clues to what has happened to a people, their moments of national glory or despair, their traditions and their history. Let us take a brief journey into Portugal's history, so that we may understand and visualize the heritage from which her folk tales have sprung.

The region formed by Spain and Portugal at the south-westernmost tip of the continent of Europe is known as the Iberian Peninsula, since it is believed that the earliest known people of this particular part of the world were the Iberians. We do not know much of the early history of the region, but we know that on it many people left their imprint. At one time the Celts journeyed there from the north; the Phoenicians, great seamen and traders, established trading posts there; and the Greeks and Carthaginians lived for a time in settlements along the coast. During the second century before Christ, Roman legions invaded Hispania (another name for the Iberian Peninsula). It remained a Roman province for several centuries. In that period the cultural foundations of this part of the world were laid.

At the beginning of the fifth century an invasion of Teutonic tribes swept down from the north. They were followed in turn by the Visigoths, who ruled for another two centuries.

Then, in 711, the Moors sailed across the narrow sea separating Africa from Europe, and captured most of the Iberian Peninsula.

The Moors—Mohammedan people of Arab and Berber stock—occupied most of what is now Spain and two thirds of what is now Portugal. In Portugal their reign lasted well over three hundred years, and in Spain even longer. Signs of their presence still exist in both countries, in the south especially. We can see the Moorish influence in the architecture, in the decorations of glazed pottery and tile, in the mosques so strange to western eyes, in the fountains and beautiful gardens, in the streets and buildings. It is natural that the long Moorish occupation is reflected in the folk tales of Spain and Portugal as well. The title story in this book, *The Little Horse of Seven Colors*, about a northern count and a Moorish princess, is an example.

By 1094 Portugal had been taken back from the Moors and entrusted to a crusading knight, Henry of Burgundy. Henry's son Alfonso I recaptured Lisbon in 1147 and won other great victories. He became Portugal's first king. When the Algarve (the southernmost part of the peninsula) was made part of Portugal in 1263 the country's boundaries were established as they remain today—the ocean to the west and south, the Spanish frontier to the north and east.

From 1499 to 1580 Portugal was a world power; her possessions and commercial enterprises reached around the globe. It was the skill and knowledge of Henry the Navigator (1349–1460) that inspired and set on their way the first of the remarkable Portuguese navigators: Diogo Cão, who discovered the Congo in 1482; Bartholomeu Dias, who rounded the Cape of Good Hope in 1487; Vasco da Gama, who sailed around Africa to India in 1498; Pedro Álvares

Cabral, who in 1500 was the first to set foot on what is now Brazil. And Ferdinand Magellan (Magalhães in Portuguese) who was the first to circumnavigate the globe. It took his ships three years, from 1519 to 1522.

Portugal is no longer a great world sea power. But her boundaries have not changed since the thirteenth century, and save for a short period between 1580 and 1640 when the royal houses of Spain and Portugal were joined by marriage, the country has maintained her independence to this day.

The soil of Portugal is fertile, its climate temperate, without extremes. More than half its people work the land, and because the country has such an extended coastline many others gain their livelihood from the sea. And so farmers and fisherman, oxen and sea perch, figure largely in the tales its people tell, as do the olives, almonds, and grapes they grow for wine. Christ, Saint Peter, the Devil, all have their place and become real and familiar. The rich man who befriends his poor neighbor, the shoemaker who cannot feed all the hungry mouths in his household and is helped out by kindly neighbors, the starving fisherman who finds a jewel in the belly of a perch, the farmer who cannot pay his rent, even the figure of Death—these are the "people next door" to the Portuguese reader. Certain of the folk tales are about the hero of the region, who is perhaps very clever or dashingly handsome, or perhaps a figure of fun, a fool. In Spain and Portugal this fun figure, more than a trifle slow-thinking and slow-moving, is Pedro de Malas-

Artes, or the *Clumsy Pedro* of this collection. There are many stories about Pedro. Much loved also are the nonsense tales, games, and repetitive dance stories that are enjoyed the world over. But perhaps Portugal's most familiar and most loved tale is that of *The Cockroach and the Mouse*, in which the cockroach is an attractive heroine whose troubles cause concern to all who read about her.

Just as we learn many things about a country's cultural background from its folk stories, so we can find insights into national traits. The Portuguese are no exception, and exemplify characteristics of which the people may well be proud —such as generosity and charity to others, and a sense of obligation to help one's neighbor in time of trouble.

This collection of twenty-eight stories was chosen from about 250 tales found in the works of three men: Teófilo Braga, Adolpho Coelho, and Zófimo Consiglieri Pedroso. These men shared the interest of a considerable number of European literary men of the ninetenth century, that of collecting folk tales, or "oral literature," as it is called. They listened wherever they could to the stories told in the different regions of the country and wrote them down without changes or improvement. Portuguese is a rich language. The people, whether they have money or not, whether they have been educated or not, have wit and intelligence; their conversation is larded with proverbs and sayings, their expressions colorful. This style and humor shines through the folk tales themselves.

Here are the folk tales of Portugal, changed only where

differences in language or custom might make them hard
to understand. We hope you will enjoy them as the people
of Portugal do, and share in the traditions of the country's
past and present.

Patricia Tracy Lowe
Anne Marie Jauss

1970

NOTES

on points of interest in the stories and illustrations

BORN TO BE RICH

page 24: Firewood is not easily obtainable in Portugal. Very often people strip off the lower branches of pine trees, because they burn so well. Bakers use this wood to heat their ovens.

page 25: The fisherwoman has tied a cord below her waist to hold her skirts up out of the way.

THE TEN DWARFS OF AUNT GREENWATER

page 29: It is customary for women to carry heavy jars or baskets on their heads. A little doughnut-shaped cushion makes their task easier.

THE PRICE OF EGGS

page 35: The older prisons in small towns permit prisoners to converse through the heavily barred windows that look out toward the street. Sometimes they even hang out little baskets on the end of a string and receive alms from passers-by.

HOW THE WILD BOARS CAME TO BE

page 39: The common breed of pig in Portugal is the razor-back, with long, reddish-brown hair and an elongated snout.

13

THE MIRACULOUS FLUTE

page 45: Vendors carry their clay pots and jars to market on the backs of mules or donkeys, well cushioned with straw and packed in large nets.

THE LEGEND OF THE ALMOND TREE

page 51: Although they exist throughout the country, the really large almond orchards are found in the Algarve, the southernmost province of Portugal.

SNOW IN THE MOUNTAINS

page 53: The old peasant is shown wearing a *sammarra*, or jacket, and a *safões*, or leggings, open in the back like a cowboy's chaps. Both are made of brown lambskin.

NO SUPPER

page 59: Shown inside the fireplace is a *fugareiro*, a little charcoal-burning stove made of clay, in which most of the cooking is done.

THE PIRA GAME

page 63: At the ancient university of Coimbra, the student's traditional costume is a black cape worn over a black suit with long coattails.

GOOD LUCK AND GREAT RICHES

page 70: Olives are still harvested by the method of beating the branches of trees with rods.

THE STRING OF LIES

page 73: The old type of beehive, still found in some regions of the country, is made from the bark of cork oak.

THE MASTER OF MAGIC AND SPELLS

page 76: The poorer folk in Portugal cannot afford guns. They hunt instead with dogs, and beat the bushes with sticks. The breed used for rabbit hunting is the *podenco*, a kind of greyhound with short, sharply pointed ears.

THE TAIL OF THE CAT

page 81: The sardine in this story is fresh from the sea; it does not come out of a can. Fresh sardines, fried or grilled, are among the cheapest and most common of foods.

PEDRO DE MALAS-ARTES

page 86: The illustration shows a typical oxcart with solid wheels. The yoke of the oxen is richly carved and painted.

page 88: As is common in the south of Portugal, Pedro's mother wears a hat over her kerchief. In the background is an old aquaduct.

The use of nets to catch birds was once common all over Europe.

GENERAL NOTES

COSTUMES

Several illustrations show the period costumes worn by men and women of Portugal at different times in the country's history. Shown also are the traditional folk costumes, which are seen only rarely today. Very elaborate, heavily embroidered dresses and jackets are, to be sure, worn during festivals—of which there are plenty in Portugal. But the black wool cap, which in some places is green with a red border, is still common in many regions of the country. Men still wrap the *faixa*, or woolen sash, around their waists. Women are often seen in a black fringed shawl in place of a coat. Sometimes they will be shod in black patent leather slippers, with wooden heels and often embroidery on the toes. Lovely gold and silver filigree jewelry worn by women is a common sight. The fishermen of Nazare still wear the brilliantly colored plaid shirts and trousers of a century or more ago. And road workers still don a coat of straw to protect them when it rains.

Money

The *escudo* is the monetary unit of the country. It is divided into one hundred centavos and is worth today roughly three and one half cents. Once it was made out of gold, and at a later time silver. A *milreis*, meaning a thousand *reis*, the plural of *real*, or "royal", was a gold coin that is now no longer used. However, it is today the monetary unit of Brazil, a Portuguese-speaking country that once belonged to Portugal. A *cruzado*, so called because a cross was depicted on it, was a gold and then a silver coin. It is no longer in existence, but the word itself still has currency, meaning it is still used, much like our "two bits" for a quarter. It is worth forty centavos.

THE LITTLE HORSE OF
SEVEN COLORS

A handsome young count, fighting in the wars against the Moors, was taken prisoner and brought before the Moorish king. The king's three daughters, who were all very beautiful, pleaded with their father to allow the count to remain with them in the palace until his ransom arrived. The king agreed.

That evening the oldest princess met the count in the castle garden and told him she would marry him if he were able to teach her something she did not know.

The prisoner answered her thus: "I will teach you about my religion, of which you are ignorant, and then we will journey to my country and marry there." But the princess would not agree to this, and went away.

A little later the second princess came to the prisoner. She

17

too told him she would marry him if he could teach her something she did not know. After listening to the same answer, she also went away.

Then came the youngest of the three princesses, and she was the most beautiful of all. Unlike her sisters, she did wish to learn of the count's religion, and listened attentively to all he told her. Then the two of them plotted to flee from the palace without the knowledge of the king.

"Go to the stables when everyone is sleeping," the girl told the count. "There you will find a little horse of seven colors. He can run as fast as thought. Wait for me there in the courtyard and we will flee together."

That night the youngest princess crept into the courtyard, clothed in her most beautiful Moorish costume with her many jewels shining in spite of the dark, and she and the count fled to the north on the back of the little horse who ran quicker than thought. No one stopped them; no one caught up with them; they did not speak. When they reached the sandy plain on the outskirts of the city where the count lived, he dismounted.

"Wait for me here," he said, "while I find you the clothes proper for an appearance at court. If you continue to dress like a Moorish princess, you will be taken prisoner in your turn."

At his words the princess wept. "Never leave me," she begged. "If you do, you will surely forget me."

"How could that be possible?" scoffed the count.

"I know it. If you leave me and go to your home, someone will embrace you and you then will forget me completely."

The count did not take her words very seriously, but he promised that he would permit no one to embrace him. He then left the sandy plain. When he arrived at his castle, he was met by his old nurse, who flung her arms around him before he could stop her. Immediately all memories of the princess waiting for him in the sandy plain left his head.

When the count did not return, the princess went to a nearby hut and was taken in and treated kindly by an old woman and her daughter. Some time later the town buzzed with the news that the count was going to marry a beautiful maiden. The Moorish princess was very sad.

Early on the day of the wedding, the princess clad herself in stable groom's clothing and took her little horse of seven colors to the square in front of the church where the wedding was to take place.

When the count arrived, surrounded by his retinue, he was astonished to see such a beautiful horse. Approaching it to see it more clearly, he heard the groom utter these words:

> "Do not forget, little horse, to trot
> And wave your mane
> As the count forgot
> His Moorish princess alone on the plain."

At once the spell was broken and the count remembered all that had happened to him. He gave orders to stop the wedding. The young stable groom standing before him was overjoyed, and told the count she was his princess. They were married soon after and were very happy.

BORN TO BE RICH

There was once a cobbler who worked night and day but was never able to fill his purse. Every day as he worked the cobbler sang the same song:

> "A cobbler am I
> Who spends all he earns.
> Born to be poor am I
> So why, tell me why
> Do I work quite so hard?"

A rich neighbor, overhearing this song, had the idea of surprising the cobbler with good fortune for a change. He sent over a cake for the cobbler to eat with his wife and children. Inside the cake some gold pieces were hidden. "He'll have little to complain about from now on," the generous neighbor told himself.

The cobbler thanked the rich man for the gift. But because he had not paid the doctor the last time one of his children was ill and so owed him money, he told his wife to take the cake to him as a present.

A few days later the rich neighbor heard the cobbler singing his same lament, and he was very surprised. "Did you and your family not eat up the cake?" he asked. The

cobbler explained that he had felt obliged to give it to the doctor.

A short time later he received another gift from the rich neighbor, this time a load of pine branches, under which a purse full of money was hidden. Now on the same street there lived a baker who had often given the cobbler bread even when he had no money. In gratitude the cobbler took the pine branches to the baker, to burn in his furnace.

When the rich neighbor passed by the cobbler's door, he asked if the branches had burned brightly, and so he heard that they had been given to the baker.

"My dear man," said the neighbor. "You are right to sing as you do, that you were born to be poor. For in the cake and under the pine branches I sent you money. Right now I can do no more, much as I would like to. All I have is this piece of lead that I found just now lying on the street."

The cobbler thanked him, shook his head at his own ill luck, and since he had no use for the lead, placed it high on a shelf. Then he went back to his stool, singing his sad tune as he worked.

That night when the household was in bed, there came a knocking at the door. "Neighbor, neighbor," said a voice. It belonged to the wife of the fisherman who lived next door. "My husband goes to sea now to fish," she said. "It will be good tonight. But he has not enough lead to weight his fishline. Have you any to give me?"

The cobbler remembered the lead given him by the rich neighbor that he had placed on the shelf. He gave it to the fisherman's wife.

The catch was good that night, and in the morning the fisherman brought to the cobbler's family a beautiful large perch. When his wife was cleaning it, she found a stone, like glass, inside its belly. Without thinking about it twice, she gave it to her children for a toy. When the little ones went to bed, the stone lay forgotten on the floor. After the cobbler blew out his candle, he caught sight of something shining at his feet like the eyes of a cat. "What is that, gleaming there?" he asked aloud, and picking the object up, he found it was a shining stone. His wife remembered that she had found it inside the fish and told her husband about it.

Next day the cobbler took the stone to a jeweler, who told him it was worth a great deal, so much that he himself could not buy it. "Only the king can afford such stones," he told the cobbler, and promised to show it at court. Immediately the king saw the stone, he wanted it for himself, and arranged to buy it from the cobbler in exchange for a great deal of money.

No longer was the cobbler's life poor and full of misery. He bought a house and a farm, and he and his family lived well. When the rich neighbor, who had been away, returned to his home and saw how the cobbler now lived, he believed he had been cheated. "He deceived me with those tales," he said to himself. "Instead he himself kept the money out of the cake and from under the pine branches."

But when the cobbler visited his old neighbor he was able to convince him of his honesty by describing how the piece of lead had brought him good fortune.

"Thank you a thousand times, neighbor," he said. "Even though I turned my back on good fortune twice, it seems I was not born to be poor, after all."

THE TEN DWARFS
OF AUNT GREENWATER

There was once a lazy woman who was unable to live in harmony with her husband because she worked little, and what she did was ill done, half done, or done not at all. At night when her man returned home he found the bed unmade, his dinner uncooked, and no water in which to wash his feet. At last he became so angry at this state of affairs that he began to beat his wife.

Unhappy about her bruises, the wife complained to her neighbor, an old woman known to all as Aunt Greenwater whom, it was told, the fairies helped.

"Oh, Aunt," sighed the wife, "perhaps you can tell me what to do."

"Certainly, my dear," replied Aunt Greenwater. "I know of ten dwarfs who are most industrious. They will come to

your house to help you for eight days. But," the old woman continued, "there are certain things you must do to ensure their assistance." And she explained that the wife must make the bed early in the day, light the fire, put the filled kettle on the hob, sweep the house, wash the linen, and while dinner cooked, wait patiently for her husband's return. "Then the dwarfs will be of help to you, even if you don't see them," said Aunt Greenwater.

The wife did exactly as she had been instructed. The day's work went well, and before dark the wife thanked her neighbor. The husband was filled with amazement at his clean and orderly house. When eight days were up without one beating, the husband told his wife that she was a changed woman, and that he was very content. She in turn was beside herself with joy, and went to thank Aunt Greenwater for her help.

"Oh, Aunt, your ten dwarfs did me a great service. Now everything goes well and these days my husband is very kind to me. Can you not arrange it so that the ten dwarfs stay with me?"

"Stay with you?" cried her neighbor. "Have you not seen them even now?"

"No, I have not. I wish I could," said the wife.

"You are a foolish one," exclaimed Aunt Greenwater, smiling at the wife. "If you want to see the dwarfs, look at the ten fingers of your hands. It is your fingers who are the dwarfs, and it is they who did the work."

The woman understood, and went back to her house, able now to do her work in happiness and without complaint.

THE VIPER AND THE
FRIAR'S ROPE

A band of friars sat at a table, eating their evening meal with great enjoyment. One of them, having consumed a large amount, wished to loosen the rope that belted his waist, but he was unwilling to reveal his discomfort. Then an idea came to him, and he said to his companions:

"Once when I was traveling in search of alms, I walked through a field. In this field there was a viper. What an enormous viper it was—it was like this—" and the friar took the rope from around his waist. He held it up to show the others, stretched between his two hands. "It was this long, more or less."

Then the friar retied the rope around him, only more loosely, and continued to eat, with the other friars none the wiser.

30

THE PRICE OF EGGS

A young man, about to sail away on a journey, to where I don't remember, passed by an inn before embarking and asked for something to eat. The mistress of the inn told him that all she could give him were boiled eggs.

"So bring me a copper's worth of those," he ordered. After eating the eggs, the young man gave the woman a cruzado and asked for change.

"I have none," she answered. "Pay me next time you pass by."

Wherever he traveled in distant lands, the young man remembered the souls of the dead in purgatory, and when he passed by a shrine he would give them alms. The devil was always shown on the shrines at the side of the dead souls, and the young man talked to them all, souls and devil as

well. "Here, souls of the dead, here's money for you, so that you will give me aid, and so you, devil, will not help me, but not hinder me either."

Several years later the young man returned to his own region. Passing by the inn where he had eaten the eggs, he went in. "I come to pay my debt," he told the mistress of the inn.

"What debt is that?" she asked.

"When I left," he explained, "I bought a copper's worth of eggs and did not pay for them." And the young man held out a copper in his hand.

"Ah yes, I remember," said the woman. "And you think you can pay for those eggs with a copper? You ate six eggs, yes? Just let me figure out what you really owe me.

Six eggs, and the hens they would have become, and their eggs . . ." and the woman continued to count until the bill added up to several hundred milreis.

The young man had little money, not nearly enough to pay this huge debt, and he was taken to prison.

A week later a stranger came to the prison and sought out the window of the young man, whom he began to question. "You have no one to defend you?" he asked through the bars. "Today at three they will sentence you. I will be your lawyer and will come to defend you."

That afternoon the young man was taken to the court. The mistress of the inn was there also. At three o'clock the stranger who was to defend the young man appeared before the judge, his face black with soot. The judge spoke to him sternly. "Why did you not wash before coming to court?" he asked.

"Because I was roasting chestnuts to sow in the ground," the young man's lawyer answered.

Then the mistress of the inn interrupted the proceedings. "Chestnut trees cannot grow from roasted chestnuts, you foolish man," she said with scorn.

"No, nor chickens from boiled eggs," said the lawyer quickly. Turning to the judge, he continued, "This young man does not owe the innkeeper as much money as she demands. She asks that he pay for chickens she would have raised from six boiled eggs. Let him go free."

The judge agreed with the lawyer and did as he asked. Who was the lawyer? The devil, of course.

THE FOOLISH LAD
AND THE FLIES

A foolish lad with a shaven scalp could not stand the bites of the flies on his head. He decided to complain about them to the judge at court. The judge came to hear the complaint only because he thought it a big joke.

"Whenever you see a fly," he pronounced to the foolish lad with a laugh, "you are permitted to defend yourself, and to give it a blow."

To make sure that he had heard aright, the lad asked the judge to repeat his words. At the moment he did so, a fly settled on the head of the judge. The foolish lad smote it mightily. The judge fell to the ground, and his attendants caught hold of the lad.

"Remember the sentence," the foolish lad reminded the judge quickly. And so they were forced to set him free. Is it true what they say, "With foolish ones, even Heaven cannot win"?

HOW THE WILD BOARS
CAME TO BE

Christ and St. Peter journeyed around the world, seeing all things and judging them. One day while they were walking along the open road, they encountered four little pigs, very young and miserable.

"Poor creatures, they must be lost," said St. Peter.

"Take them in your care, Peter," said Christ, "for assuredly they have no master. We'll pass a house soon, I am certain, and we will give them to those within to look after."

St. Peter was cautious, and he remembered the advice of the proverb: "If you are given a little pig, make sure it doesn't escape you." So he cut himself a switch from a bush beside the road and drove all four pigs in front of him.

At last they came to a farmhouse, where a woman stood at the door. St. Peter proposed a bargain to her. "Take good

care of these little animals," he said, "and when we return a year from now, you will keep two of them and we will take two with us."

The woman agreed. In no time at all the little pigs grew big and fat, already worth a great deal at the market.

When the year was over, Christ and St. Peter came once more to the farmhouse. When the woman saw them approaching, she hid the fattest of the pigs in the sty.

"Here are the pigs," she said, opening the door in answer to St. Peter's knock. "Only two remain. The others sickened and died, only last week."

The Divine Master looked searchingly at the women and said, "I know well what you have done. Here is my verdict. These two alone we will divide between us. Those you have hidden away, the strongest and the fattest, will go free to the mountains, to hunt their forests as fierce wild boars."

BOLA BOLA

In a house near the wood where the king hunted lived three sisters who were very fond of each other. In the depths of the wood itself lived a witch who hated the sisters and the happiness they enjoyed together; in particular she hated the beauty of the youngest sister. The witch plotted against them all.

One day she brought a sprig of coriander to the youngest girl and said to her, "Give this to your sisters tonight in their soup. It will make it taste very good. But take care not to eat of it yourself."

The innocent girl did as she was told, and when her sisters ate their soup they changed into cows. Sorrowfully the girl lived with her strange-looking sisters and tried to treat them as before, giving them the same food she ate herself.

A day or two later, when the king was out hunting, he caught sight of the young girl. At once he was enamored of her beauty and took her as his queen. The two cows went with their sister to live in the palace. The witch was furiously angry at the good fortune of the sisters, and promised herself further revenge.

She bided her time until the youngest sister, now the queen, gave birth to a fine son. After the king had left for the hunt, the witch entered the chamber of the queen. "Poor lady, you are ill," she said, and putting her hand to the queen's brow, she pierced her temples with two sharp pins. The queen, bewitched in her turn, changed into a dove and flew away.

The witch hid herself in the royal bed. "What has become of your great beauty?" asked the king on his return.

"It is gone, for the while, because I am ill," answered the witch. The king believed her and treated her as his wife, and so they lived for some time. Unknown to the king the witch ordered that the two cows be given hay to eat, instead of the fine food provided before by their sister. It was not long before they began to starve.

Now in the palace there was a small talking dog by the name of Bola Bola. The queen had been very fond of this dog, and after she had changed into a dove she came to visit him each day.

"Bola Bola," she would call.

"What does my lady wish?" the talking dog answered.

"I wish to know how my young son is, with his new nurse," said the dove.

"At night he is quiet, but during the day he cries," Bola
Bola told her.

This conversation took place so often that it was heard by
others in the palace and at last the king learned about it.
He ordered that the dove be brought before him. Holding
her in his hands, and smoothing the feathers of her head,
he felt the two pins and pulled them out. Once again his
lovely young queen stood before him. The king, hearing the
whole story from her, banished the witch from his king
dom forever, after ordering her to restore the cows to their
rightful form. Then he and the queen and her two sisters
lived happily together.

THE MIRACULOUS FLUTE

One time when Christ was journeying through the world accompanied by St. Peter, they passed an orange grove watched over by a young boy. It was a hot day, without a breeze, and St. Peter was very thirsty. "An orange would certainly taste good," he said. "Would you let me eat one, my lad?"

"Pick one at your pleasure," answered the boy. St. Peter had nothing to give the boy in payment. But he knew Christ would reward the lad somehow, should he eat an orange also, and he suggested to Christ that he too should quench his thirst.

To the second request the lad answered cheerfully, "Pick, master, as many as you wish."

The Divine Master, as Peter had guessed, wished to re-

pay this generous goodwill, and he asked the boy, "Do you
desire your salvation?"

"Yes, of course, sir," replied the lad. "But first I'd like to
have a flute that makes everyone dance when I play it."

Christ gave the boy his flute and went away with St.
Peter. And the boy, forgetting all about his job, entertained
himself by playing the flute.

The owner of the orange grove, who had been hiding in
a thicket of brambles nearby and was about to scold the
boy for his laziness, instead began to dance. He could not
stop dancing, and the brambles scratched and tore at his
legs and clothes.

Pleased with his new powers, the boy went toward town.
On the way he passed a vendor, his mule loaded with pottery to sell at the market. At the sound of the flute the mule
began to dance. Everything jigged up and down, vendor,

mule, and pottery alike. The man, angered when his wares lay broken on the ground, grabbed hold of the boy and took him into the town and before a judge for punishment.

Hearing the facts of the boy's naughtiness, the judge frowned. "Where is this flute?" he asked. "I must see for myself what it can do." When he saw the simple reed, he was sure he was being hoodwinked. "Play," he ordered in angry disbelief.

The boy took back the flute and played. The judge, his clerk, the table, the books, even the vendor, all danced in a frenzy. Everything in the courtroom whirled about and could not stop. In the middle of the hubbub the judge's mother, who had lain ill next door for seven years, entered the room, dancing and singing and clapping her hands.

> "Let us dance the wild *folia,*
> See me dance the wild *folia,*
> I who for seven years
> Have lain flat on my back."

The judge marveled at the sight. Breathlessly he asked the boy to stop playing. The lad obeyed instantly.

Wiping his brow, the judge said to him, "Go in peace. You made trouble and damage with your flute, but I will pay for the things you have broken, for you cured my mother, who for seven long years could not walk a step. Use your flute wisely, from now on."

THE SHOEMAKER

The shoemaker sat on his stool before the door to his house and worked the day long. And all day long he sang. He had many children to feed and was so poor he could only clothe them in rags. But he was content, and at night when his wife cooked their meager meal the shoemaker played his fiddle and the children danced around him.

A rich man in the town had taken note of the shoemaker's sorry life, and took pity on him, sending over a bag of money.

The shoemaker was astonished. That evening he locked his door and sat with his wife to count the coins that were in the bag of money. He forgot his fiddle. His children played noisily indoors, closed in by the locked door, and the shoemaker made mistakes in his counting. So he beat the children, who cried and cried, louder by far than when they had cried from hunger.

"What shall we do with so much money?" asked the wife.

"We will bury it," was her husband's reply.

"But we couldn't get at it then. Let us hide it in the chest."

"There it can be stolen," the shoemaker objected. "Let us lend it out, and ask for interest."

"That is usury," his wife said knowingly.

"Then I'll enlarge our rooms, perhaps add a story to the house. I'll paint it fresh; yes, and fix up my workshop," said the shoemaker.

"All that will achieve is to make more work for me," grumbled the wife. "Let us buy fields. I am the daughter of a farmer and I need land to till."

"That interests me not in the least," was her husband's answer.

"It is owning land that counts," she went on, paying no attention. "Nothing else is of importance."

The two of them argued on through the night, until the man was so angry that he slapped his wife and she returned the favor. Neither slept a wink, and next morning they did not speak to each other.

The rich man across the way observed the change at once, and he could not understand what had happened to his cheerful shoemaker.

At last, near the noon hour, the shoemaker spoke to his wife. "It is the money that is responsible. It made our old happiness fly out of the window. It would be best, I think, to give it back to our neighbor, so our old poverty, which kept us close together, will be with us once again."

The woman hugged the husband in her joy and he, eager to recover the contentment of the whole family, returned the purse whence it came.

Once more the shoemaker sat on his stool before the door, smiling and singing as he sewed.

THE LEGEND OF THE ALMOND TREE

They say the almond tree outwitted the Devil. Thus it is remarkable among trees, for as well it is the first to bloom and its fruits the last to ripen.

Astonished at seeing almond blossoms one day in January, the Devil sat down in the tree's shade to wait for the nuts to ripen. He was content, thinking that after he had harvested all the almonds he wanted there would be time to move on to other trees and watch their blossoms turn into fruit for him to eat. From January to September he waited and waited. Tired at last of sitting under the still unripened almonds, he left to find other fruits to eat.

But once again the Devil met disappointment. For by September all the other fruit had been harvested. Returning angrily to the almond tree, the Devil discovered that here too he'd been cheated of his meal, for in his absence every almond had been picked.

SNOW IN THE MOUNTAINS

A king, planning to test the wisdom of his counselors, took them for a walk. Passing an old man working in a field, the king greeted him.

"Much snow in the mountains," he said.

The old man grinned. "'Tis true, and it's the time for it," he replied.

The counselors looked at one another, completely bewildered, for it was in the heat of summer.

"Did your house burn down, and how many times?" the king went on.

"Yes, sir, it did, and twice," came the answer.

"And how many more times will you be fleeced?" asked the king.

"Still three more times," replied the old man.

The counselors listened in astonishment as the king continued to talk to the old man.

"When three ducks next come to you, be sure to pluck them," he ordered.

"I will do so, if you order it, sir," agreed the old man.

The king and his counselors went on their way. "You understand nothing," mocked the king. "If you cannot explain what the old man and I were talking about, you will no longer be my counselors, for you are not fit for it," and he left them behind.

The three men, hoping to keep both their reputation for wisdom and their post as king's counselors, went to the old man himself for the answers.

"I will explain all," he told them, "if you will take off

your clothes and give them to me, together with all the money you are carrying."

The counselors had little choice. When they had done as the old man asked, he said to them:

" 'Much snow in the mountains'?" He pointed to his head. "It is because I have white hair and plenty of it. 'It's the time for it,' means I'm well along in years. 'Did your house burn down, and how many times?' You remember the proverb 'Your house burns down each time you marry a daughter.' This means that a father spends much to give a girl away. I know what it costs, for I've married two. 'How many more times will you be fleeced?' Three times, for I still have three daughters yet unwed, and there is the proverb 'Who marries off his daughter is fleeced of his money.' As for the three ducks, why, that is you three gentlemen, who kindly gave me your clothing and money in exchange for my explanation."

The counselors had no time to take out their anger on the old man, for the king appeared once again and said to them, "If you wish to regain your clothing and money and return to your position in the palace, you must give the old man a dowry and wedding costs for each of his daughters that remain. Learning his wisdom is a costly matter, counselors."

THE TIPSY ROOSTER

A tipsy rooster, climbing a hill one day to scratch for worms, found a purse lying on the ground. It was filled with money.

"I shall take this purse to the king," said the rooster to himself, and he set out with it in his beak. After a while he came to a river, which he could not cross. Still holding the purse, he opened his beak just a little and said, "O river, retreat, so that I may walk to the other side." But the river paid no attention, and so the rooster drank up all its water and walked on.

A little further on the rooster met a fox on the road. "Let me pass," he said, but the fox did not budge and the rooster gobbled him up.

Walking on, the rooster came to a pine tree growing up in the middle of the path. "Out of my way, pine," said the rooster. "I wish to pass." But the pine just swayed in the wind, and the rooster ate it up.

Further on, the tipsy rooster encountered a wolf, and then an owl. Both of them he ate when they would not stir at his command.

Arriving at the castle, the rooster asked to be received by the king, and gave him the purse. The king ordered the rooster placed in the royal chicken coop along with the palace chickens. Even though he was well treated, the rooster did not like being shut up at all. He began to crow:

> "Cockadoodledoo,
> Bring my purse back to me."

When no one returned the purse, the rooster opened his beak very wide and out jumped the fox and ate up all the palace chickens. When the king heard what had happened, he ordered that the rooster be locked up in a cupboard. Inside the cupboard, which was full of glassware, the rooster began to crow:

> "Cockadoodledoo,
> Bring my purse back to me."

But no one returned the purse. So the rooster opened his beak very wide once again, and out fell the pine tree, breaking the glasses and everything else that was in the cupboard.

"Shut him up in the stable with the horses," shouted the king, furious with rage.

"Cockadoodledoo,
    Bring my purse back to me,"

crowed the rooster, and when nothing happened, he let out the wolf who ate up all the horses.

When the king ordered him to be placed in a jar of oil, the rooster opened his beak, and out jumped the owl and drank up all the oil.

By this time the king was at his wits' end. "Into the oven with him," he roared.

"Cockadoodledoo,
    Bring my purse back to me,"

crowed the rooster, and opening his beak, he let out the river. Seeing his castle already half under water, the king ordered that the purse should be quickly returned to the rooster before they all drowned.

With the purse safely in his beak once more, the tipsy rooster took to the road again.

NO SUPPER

There is truth in the old proverb:

> He with many children
> And not a crust of bread
> Takes each one by the hand
> And sings him a song instead.

A man with little money to support his six children met further misfortune with the sudden death of his wife. Neighbors who learned of his misery tried to help by adding their bit to his daily earnings, and the man determined to keep his family together. The poor man's heart was heavy, however, as they crowded around his chair before the empty grate. One cried; one begged him for bread; and another told him he could hardly stand, he was so hungry.

To stop their tears, the poor man played a game of hope with them. "Today there was no one to bake us any bread," he said. "But let us have patience. Fortune is like the wind, forever changing its direction. Who knows, tomorrow I may be roasting a sheep for our supper."

The little ones licked their lips. "Oh Father, give me a piece of the shank," said one.

"Of course, my son," the man replied. "With two potatoes as well."

"And I, I would like . . ." began another, so weak with hunger his words came slowly.

"Stew," interrupted a third. "That would be good, lamb stew, with a bowl of gravy to soak up the bread."

"You shall have large slices," the father assured him.

"And I," said the smallest child, "I will have shank, and stew, and bread to crumble in it."

"Listen to him, Father," objected the first. "It isn't enough for him to have roast. He wants everything else as well."

"Potatoes for me, Father?" the second managed to ask.

"Not my potatoes, Father," complained the smallest, beginning to cry.

"Don't worry, my children," said their father hastily. "We will make a fine rice dish with the heart and the liver."

"Oh, how good!" said the youngest child, comforted once more. "I like that so much."

"Will you give me rice, too?" asked the second child.

"A whole plate of it?" said the oldest.

"It goes without saying," the father assured them all. "But now it is time to be quiet and go to sleep. Sleep well, my little ones."

Soon all was hushed in that mourning home of need and sorrow. The children's happy dreams of food had filled their empty stomachs.

And the kindly neighbors, overhearing the talk of roast
lamb and stew, whispered among themselves, "Let us make
it come true. Let us take up a collection, and take the little
children their roast lamb and stew, and potatoes and rice."

THE PIRA GAME

A student with very little money in his pocket was traveling around the countryside. Stopping one day at an inn, he planned how to eat without paying for his meal. The student asked the innkeeper for everything he desired, and after he had eaten well, he carried out his plan of escape.

"I will teach you a new game," he told the mistress of the inn.

"What is this game?" she asked the student.

"Hold this ball of yarn," he replied, picking it up from where he had spied it on the table. "And I will tie the end around my thumb. This is called the pira game. You'll see how it is played." And the student started to pull on the ball of yarn, walking backward toward the door and calling "pira, pira, pira," to the mistress of the inn.

She, in her turn, allowed the ball of wool to unwind in her hands, and stared at the student as he continued to call "pira, pira, pira." Once outside the inn door and on the street, he turned and began to run, still crying "pira, pira, pira, pira down here." But no one was able to catch him.

AUNT MISERY

There once was an old woman clothed in tatters and in utter need. One would think she'd been born when the world began, she seemed so old. She was known to all around as Aunt Misery. This old woman lived in a hut, with walls of stone from the field, and a roof of straw and branches from the woods. Her one possession, which she prized greatly, was a pear tree that grew in front of her door. Unhappily, all too often this tree was under attack by the village boys, who climbed it, damaged it, and robbed it of its fruit.

One day a pilgrim came to the old woman's door and asked her for shelter. Aunt Misery gave him all she had— the blanket she threw over herself at night, and the only crust of bread in the house. At daybreak the pilgrim pre-

64

pared to leave, but first he bade Aunt Misery make a request, which would be granted her.

Aunt Misery's needs were small. "One thing I ask for, and nothing more," she said.

"Whatever pleases you, little aunt, ask me for it," the pilgrim said to her.

"I ask that whoever climbs my pear tree cannot descend unless I order it."

"Your wish will be granted," the stranger assured her as he went on his way.

The boys of the village knew nothing of what had happened, but very soon they felt the effect of the pilgrim's marvelous gift. From high in the pear tree's branches they called out to Aunt Misery, begging her to allow them to descend.

"Only if you promise never to climb my tree again," she replied. The boys were happy to agree, and from that day on the fruit remained safe on the branches, waiting for Aunt Misery to pick it.

All went well, until one day another stranger stopped at Aunt Misery's door. Unlike the first, however, he appeared sinister to her, and foreboding.

"What do you want?" Aunt Misery asked.

"I am Death, who has come for you," was the reply.

"Already? Grant me another small year, at least."

"It cannot be," answered the stranger.

"Then let me eat that one pear on my tree, which hangs there forgotten," said the old woman.

"That I will permit you."

"Then do me the favor of climbing to pick it, so that I may eat it," said Aunt Misery.

The stranger climbed the pear tree's branches, and quickly the old woman made use of her wonderful gift.

"Remain there, Death, until I order you down," she pronounced.

And so it happened that for a time no one died in the land, until at last Death offered a bargain to Aunt Misery. He would spare her life, if she permitted him to climb down from the pear tree to take care of others. The old woman agreed. And that is why misery is forever present in the world.

GOOD LUCK AND GREAT RICHES

A poor man worked in the forest, cutting wood and selling the logs in the town to support his wife and children. One day he looked up from his work and saw beside him two women clad in costly garments.

"We are Good Luck and Great Riches," one of them said to him, "and we have come to help you." Turning away from the woodcutter, the two women commenced to argue over his head, each one sure that she was best able to be of help to the poor man.

"Being rich is everything," said Great Riches. "Only I can help him."

"But I will bring him good luck, even without riches," said the other. "My way is best for him. I give by far the greater benefit."

"Let us carry out an experiment, then," said Great Riches, turning to the woodcutter. "Take this cruzado," she said to him, "and tomorrow do no work. Instead buy meat, bread, and wine, and rest with your family and eat."

The poor woodcutter went home very content. Next day he walked to the butcher, giving him his cruzado before choosing his meat. The shop was very noisy, however, filled with people and confusion. The butcher did not remember that the woodcutter had already paid him, and the poor man finally gave up arguing about it and returned to the forest to chop wood.

Great Riches saw him working. When she heard what had happened to the cruzado, she was angry and fearful of losing the test, so she gave him a purse filled with doubloons.

The woodcutter began his journey to his home. The purse he had been given was made of red leather, and this caught the eye of a hawk up in the sky. Down it swooped, seized the purse in its claws, and flew away. Sadly the man told his wife what had happened, and next morning as usual went to his work in the forest.

Once more Great Riches appeared before him. When she learned what had happened to the man and the purse, she became even more desperate. "This time," she told him, "I will give you a sack of money so heavy you cannot even lift it, and I'll give you a horse as well, to help carry the money to your house."

The woodcutter thanked Great Riches for her gift, and started homeward. The lane he took passed close to a field where a mare was grazing. The man's horse began to bolt after the mare, he could not hold the horse, and mare and horse and money all vanished from his sight. Look as he might, he could not find them.

This time Great Riches did not expect to find the wood-cutter at work in the forest, but she went to the usual place to crow over Good Luck. She was greatly astonished, there-fore, to find not only her rival but the poor man working as before.

"Now it is my turn to try and make this poor man happy," said Good Luck. "I will give him a copper coin only. Here you are, woodcutter. Take this copper, and when you reach town, buy with it the first thing you see."

On his way to his home in the town, the poor man met a farmer, who said he would sell for a copper a rod to hit the

olive trees so the olives would fall and be harvested. The
woodcutter bought the rod, and next day went to the olive
grove. But when he beat with the rod the first olive tree he
saw, a red purse filled with doubloons fell from its branches.
Quickly the woodcutter snatched up the purse and took it
home to his wife, telling her from whence he believed it
came. The wife was so happy the money was found that
she vowed to make a pilgrimage of thanks. She and the
woodcutter started out. Noticing horse tracks along the path,
the man and his wife followed them, and soon came upon
the horse given him by Great Riches, with the sack of coins
still on its back. They led the horse back to their house, and
from that day on were able to live in comfort and contentment.

This time, when Great Riches and Good Fortune went to the forest in search of the woodcutter, they waited in vain. At nightfall Good Luck declared herself the winner. "What did I tell you?" she said to her rival. "It is good fortune one can be happy with, not riches."

Perhaps she was right, for without the good luck of buying the rod to harvest olives, the woodcutter would not have found the purse, the horse, or the sack of doubloons. But perhaps Great Riches was the winner, for it was her money, after all, which changed the man's life from one of need and bitterness to one of ease. Who do you think was the winner? Does Good Luck or Great Riches bring happiness to people?

THE STRING OF LIES

A farmer, unable, because of a bad harvest, to pay the rent that he owed, went to his noble landlord and asked if this time he might be excused. But the noble did not believe his tale of woe for a minute.

"I will excuse you the rent," he said, "only if you can tell me a string of lies as long as today and tomorrow."

The poor man had no idea how to satisfy his landlord, who might well put him out on the street. He went home and told his wife and son what had happened.

"Let me go to the noble landlord, Father," said the young man. "I'm sure I can convince him to forgive us the rent we owe."

"But you are such a blockhead, you never get anything straight," answered the farmer.

"Exactly. That is why I'll succeed," his son replied, and off he went.

"I've come about the rent," he said at his landlord's gate, and was taken before him.

"You know, sire," he began, "that our harvest was bad. But that's not the worst of it. My father has so many hives that he has lost track of the number of bees in them. Two days ago he counted, and concluded that one was missing. With his ax on his shoulder, he went in search of this bee. He found it in the fork of a great alder, and he cut the tree down to capture it. The bee was laden with honey and he took the honey away, but couldn't find anything to put it in. He put his hand inside his shirt and caught two fleas, made two bags out of their skins to contain the honey, and went on home. When he entered his house, a hen met him and ate the bee. My father grabbed the hen to kill it, but his ax got lost in its feathers. The flames in my father's fireplace leaped out and burned up the feathers, and my father found the axhead once more. He took it to the blacksmith for repair, and the smith made a fishhook for him . . ."

By this time the lad was almost out of breath, but he continued, "Then my father took the hook to the river to fish, and caught an old packsaddle. He threw it back and caught a donkey, who still blinked his eyes although dead for three days. My father jumped on its back and returned to the smith, who gave him a medicine for the donkey made out of the juice of dried beans. A drop of this medicine fell into the beast's ear and a bean field sprang up, which produced so many beans that I have brought fifteen carts loaded with them to pay the rent to my noble landlord."

The nobleman was exhausted with listening to such monstrous nonsense. "My lad, your lies are as many as the teeth in your mouth," he said.

"Thank you, my lord," answered the boy. "So then our rent is paid."

THE MASTER OF MAGIC
AND SPELLS

A poor farmer had three sons. The two older ones worked hard in the fields, but the youngest set himself to learning the art of magic, spells, and clever tricks.

One day the older boys said to their father, "We work hard to support the family, but our brother does not contribute even a penny. It is time he put that studying of his to some use."

Nothing loath to show off his skills, the youngest son asked his father for the collar of a dog. "I will turn myself into a hunting dog," he explained. "So you must also have a leash to hold me by, and a stick with which to beat the bushes. You'll see, we'll catch many rabbits, and afterwards we'll pass by the door of that merchant who is always boasting to you of his hunting."

The father did as his son requested, placing the dog collar around his neck. Immediately the lad turned into a beautiful hound. Together they hunted and caught many rabbits as the boy had foretold. The father walked with them strung onto his stick, and the hound padded along behind him.

When the boastful merchant saw them passing his door, he called out, "My good fellow, did you catch all that game with just one dog?"

"That's right," answered the poor farmer.

"Then I must have that dog. Will you sell him to me?"

"If you pay one hundred milreis for him you can have him" was the answer.

"Then sold he is, and to me," said the merchant happily, handing over the money to the farmer and receiving the dog in exchange. The farmer counted his money carefully and went home.

That evening the merchant went hunting in his turn and took the beautiful hound with him. Seeing a rabbit, the dog ran after it through a bramble hedge and was lost to sight. On the other side of the hedge the dog loosened his collar, and stood there once more as the farmer's youngest son.

The merchant grew very tired calling for his dog to return. He waited and waited. When the lad came from behind the brambles, the merchant said to him, "Have you seen a dog anywhere?"

"No," answered the lad politely. "But I did hear something moving in that hedge there. It is so dense, perhaps it is an animal that cannot get out," and he went on his way. The merchant, having lost both his money and the dog, was left with nothing.

Home once more, the youngest son said to his father, "I am going to change into a horse, so you must buy a bridle for me."

The poor farmer bought the bridle and put it on his son, who immediately turned into a horse. The father then rode the horse through the streets of the town.

The Master of Magic and Spells from Paris, who had

taught the boy all his skills, happened to catch sight of the horse with the farmer on its back, and of course he knew right away who it was. He approached the farmer, and told him he'd buy the horse at any price. Before the man could reply, the Master of Magic pulled a large sum from his pocket and without even looking at it, let alone counting it, handed it to the poor farmer, who was more than satisfied. In exchange, the Master of Magic led the horse off and put it in his stable, where, because the bit had not been removed from between its teeth, the horse could not eat.

Now the Master of Magic told his three daughters not under any circumstances to enter the stables. Of course, as soon as he had left the house, they said to each other, "Let us see what there is in the stable that we are forbidden to enter." Inside they saw a beautiful horse, very strongly built, who could not eat even a blade of hay because of the bit in its mouth.

"The poor horse. Let us remove the bit, maybe it is hungry," said one of the daughters, and they removed the bridle and bit.

"Let me become a bird," said the horse quickly, and right away turned into a bird and flew out of the window.

But the bird flew right under the nose of the Master of Magic, who was just then approaching the stable. He recognized the bird at once, and said, "Let me become a hawk," and flew after the bird to kill it.

Seeing the hawk close behind him, the bird said quickly, "Let me become a ring," and fell into the ocean, where a sea perch, swimming by, swallowed him up.

The perch swam through many waters, until caught by a fisherman in a distant land. The fisherman sold the perch to the palace. While the princess was in the kitchen watching, a servant cleaned the fish for cooking, saw the ring, washed it off, and gave it to the princess. She in her turn liked this ring more than any of her jewels, and put it on her finger.

That night, before going to bed, she took off the ring, placing it on a table. When it was dark, the ring changed into the youngest son, who began to address the princess. She was very frightened at this and called out to the king her father to come to her aid. In a second the lad turned into an ant, and when the king entered his daughter's room, he saw nothing.

This happened for three nights. On the third night the

youngest son spoke again to the princess.

"I am the ring you like to wear on your finger, for I am skilled in magic and spells. Because I have this wisdom, I am aware that your father the king is very ill. Your court doctors cannot cure him. Only the Master of Magic from Paris will know how to make him well. Tell your father to ask for him. The Master will not demand money or jewels in payment; only the ring you wear will satisfy him. Please do not hand the ring to him, Princess. Instead, let it drop to the floor." The young man vanished and once more the ring lay on the table. The princess placed it on her finger and went to see her father.

When the king said he was very ill, she told him the story, and the Master of Magic from Paris was summoned to cure him. As his reward, he demanded the princess's ring. Remembering what the lad had asked, the princess pretended to be angry, and threw the ring on the floor.

"Let me be grain," said the ring, and grains of millet scattered all over the floor.

The Master of Magic turned into a hen, and began to peck at the grain. But the lad turned into a weasel, sunk his teeth in the neck of the hen, and killed it. Then he changed himself back into a handsome young man and explained to the king everything that had gone before. Because he had summoned the man who had cured the king, and was therefore responsible, the king gave to the youngest son the hand of his daughter in marriage. The poor farmer's youngest son was very happy, and his family rejoiced at his good fortune.

THE TAIL OF THE CAT

There was once a cat who went to the barber for a shave. The barber said to the cat, "You would look so much more handsome if your tail were a mite shorter."

"All right, cut it a little bit," replied the cat, and the barber snipped off his tail. The cat had not long left the shop before he said to himself, "I left my tail at the barber's. I must go back and ask for it."

Once again inside the shop, the cat said to the barber, "Give me my tail, or I will make off with one of your razors." Since the barber would not give back the tail, the cat took a razor and went walking in the street.

A little further on he came to a fish seller who had lost her fish knife. "Here, have my razor," said the cat to her, and walked on.

Then the cat said to himself, "I have left the razor behind," and he returned to the fish seller. "Give me my razor, or I'll make off with one of your sardines." Since the fish seller would not give back his razor, the cat took a sardine and went walking in the street.

Further on he met a miller, sitting on a stone and eating a dry piece of bread. "Here, have this sardine," said the cat, and walked on. Then the cat said to himself, "I have left my sardine behind," and returned to the miller.

"Give me my sardine," he said, "or I'll make off with a bag of flour." Since the miller had already eaten the sardine, the cat took the sack of flour and continued his walk.

Further on, he met a teacher who had no lunch for the girls in her care. "Take this flour," he said to the teacher, and walked on. Then the cat said to himself, "I have left my sack of flour," and he went back to the teacher. "Give me back my flour, or I'll make off with one of your girls."

Since the teacher had used the flour, the cat walked on with the girl. Soon he met a washerwoman, washing her laundry in the stream. "You cannot do all that washing alone," he said to her. "Take this girl to help you." He continued his walk, but soon he remembered the girl and returned. "Give me back the girl, or I'll make off with a shirt," he told the washerwoman. Taking the shirt, he walked on.

Further on, the cat met a violin player sitting without a shirt in the hot sun. "Take this shirt, poor soul," he said. While the violin player was putting on the shirt, the cat made off with the violin, and continued until he came to a tree. He climbed it, began to play the violin, and sang this song:

"From my tail I got me a razor
From the razor I got me a sardine
From the sardine I got me some flour
From the flour I got me a girl
From the girl I got me a shirt
From the shirt I got me a violin.
Strum, strum, strum, strum,
I am a clever cat."

PEDRO DE MALAS ARTES, OR CLUMSY PEDRO

A poor widow had a son who was not a bit clever. Since he never did anything right, everyone in the village called him Clumsy Pedro. The widow had no other children, and of course she loved Pedro very much. The two of them were so poor there was never any money to buy new clothes. The widow could only darn, or put patches on those they had.

One day she brought home a square of linen cloth. "See, Pedro, this cloth will cover our holes." Soon after, she left her son to go to church. While she was gone, Pedro took the linen, cut it into small pieces, and tacked them up over the holes and cracks in the walls of their hut. When his mother returned from mass, Pedro said to her with satisfaction, "Look, Mother, how I have covered our holes!"

The widow gazed at the silly thing her son had done and

84

raised her hands to heaven in despair. She felt like packing up and leaving the house for good, but she soon thought better of it.

Next day she sent Pedro to market, telling him to buy a young pig and bring it home. She waited and waited, but her son did not return, and at last she went to look for him. Some way off from the house she caught sight of him, lying in the middle of the road with the pig on top of him. He had attempted to carry it, it appeared, and found the animal too heavy for him. The widow cried out in amazement, and then scolded her son.

"What should I have done then, Mother dear?" Pedro asked her.

"You should have tied a string around its foot and driven

it ahead of you with a stick," she explained. Clumsy Pedro listened to her carefully.

Time passed. One day the widow instructed her son to go again to market, to buy a jug. Pedro returned early this time, but with the handle only.

"Whatever happened, Pedro?" asked his mother, horrified. "Where is the jug I told you to buy and bring home?"

"I did just what you told me," the boy answered. "I tied a string to the jug, and pushed it ahead of me with a stick."

Once again the widow threw up her hands and despaired. "If you had any sense at all, you'd have carried the jug," she said. "Or if it was heavy, you could have rested it on a cart filled with straw that was coming our way." Clumsy Pedro listened carefully once again.

Another time the widow sent her son to a shop for twenty pence worth of needles. Pedro bought the needles. On the way home he passed a cart filled with straw that was going his way. Remembering his mother's instructions, he thrust the needles into the straw, and reached home ahead of the

cart. At the house his mother asked for the needles.

"They're on their way, in that load of straw our neighbor's bringing. I put them there, as you told me."

By this time Pedro's mother was good and tired of her blundering son, and resolved not to send him on any more errands.

One evening the widow bought tripe for their supper, and said to Pedro, "Take the tripe and wash it in the river, and don't return until all of it is really clean." She had forgotten all about her resolution.

"How will I know when it is clean?" the boy asked.

"Anyone will tell you," his mother answered. "Just ask someone nearby."

So the boy washed the tripe in the river. Then he washed them again. And as no one was passing, he washed them some more. Suddenly he noticed a sailboat a long way off. The men in it were forced to row, for there was no wind. Pedro waved at them.

Thinking the lad was stranded or in some sort of trouble, they bent to the oars and rowed toward him against the current. As they drew near, Pedro shouted, "Can you gentlemen tell me if these tripe are clean?"

The men in the boat were incensed with Pedro. Reaching the shore, they jumped from the boat; each one boxed the boy's ears, and then they said to him, "What you should have said to us was, 'May a strong wind fill your sails.'"

Pedro walked on toward his home, and on the way passed a field where laborers were gathering the sheaves of wheat and piling them into shocks. Pedro called out to them, "What you need is a good strong wind. May you have a strong wind."

The reapers in the field were extremely angry with Pedro and gave him a beating, saying, "You idiot boy, don't you know that a strong wind would scatter the wheat all around? It is the opposite that we need, that nothing make the shocks fall. That's what you should have said, that nothing make them fall." And they let him go.

Pedro continued on his way until he came to a place where men were putting up a net to catch the birds.

"What you need is for nothing to make them fall. I hope none of them falls," Pedro shouted at the men.

Thinking that the boy meant no bird should fall into the net, the men set about him with sticks. As they hit him, they cried, "You should say to us, 'May there be much blood,'" and they let him go.

Further on Pedro came to a path where two men were fighting, watched by several others.

"May there be much blood," Pedro told them in a loud voice. Of course, he was attacked once again and beaten with sticks. "You should have said, 'May God separate them,'" he was told.

Pedro went on his way and came to a large crowd surrounding a bride and groom fresh from the church.

"May God separate them," Pedro shouted. The wedding guests were so angry at Pedro that they slapped at him with their hands.

"'May there be many days like this one,' you should have said," was their advice.

Further on, Pedro approached the funeral of a man held in high esteem. "May there be many days like this one," the unfortunate boy called out. All who followed the coffin fell on Pedro to take a whack at him. " ' May our Lord take him straight to Heaven,' you should have said," they told him.

Poor Clumsy Pedro had long since walked right past his own cottage. When he came to a group of people leaving the church after a baptism, he called out in a loud voice, "May our Lord take him straight to Heaven."

The godparents of the baby took Pedro's words as a bad omen, and set about him with a will. Pedro fled from them down the road. And if he is not safely home with his mother, he is still roaming the world having his ears boxed by those he meets.

CLARINHA

There was once a queen who alone governed her land. It was her plan to hand over her rule to her beautiful young daughter Clarinha when the girl was old enough to marry the prince to whom she had been betrothed in childhood.

Each morning the lovely Clarinha walked in the palace garden. One day an eagle flew over her head, calling "Clarinha, Clarinha!" The girl stopped to look at him, strangely frightened.

"Which would you prefer, little princess, to work hard in your youth, or when you grow old?" Without waiting for an answer, the eagle flew away into the blue sky.

Clarinha told the queen her mother about the eagle's question. "If I were you," advised her mother, "I'd say 'I prefer to work when I am young and strong,' for to work in old age is hard."

Next day Clarinha walked in her garden more timidly than usual, and again the eagle flew overhead. When he repeated his question, the girl answered, "When I am young." No sooner had the words left her mouth than the eagle swooped down, grasped her in his talons, and flew high in the sky until he came to the country of the prince to whom Clarinha was betrothed. The girl was terrified. The eagle set Clarinha down on the ground and flew away.

Now Clarinha knew no one in this strange land save the queen and her son the prince. She realized no one would even allow her in the palace grounds, let alone into the presence of the queen or prince to ask them for help. So when she saw a bakery, she went inside and asked for work. The woman took her on, and the young girl worked hard from morning till night.

One day the woman went out, leaving Clarinha to put the kneaded loaves in the oven. Clarinha had not forgotten about the eagle, and fearful of being alone, she closed the doors to the bakery, and all the windows. But the eagle came down the chimney. His wings made a great noise as he flew around the room, breaking mixing bowls and dishes, and scattering live coals on top of the newly risen loaves of bread. He left the same way he had come. When the woman returned, she beat Clarinha for the havoc in her bakery, and since she did not believe a word of the girl's story, although Clarinha wept and pleaded with her, she turned her out into the street.

Clarinha next found work in a nearby tavern. One day the man went out, leaving her in charge. Again the girl feared the eagle would enter the tavern somehow, and she locked everything up tight. Nevertheless, the eagle succeeded in forcing an entry. Once inside, he broke the bottles of wine and all the glasses, and he opened the spigots on the barrels so that the wine poured out unchecked. Then he disappeared. When the man returned to find the inside of his tavern in ruins, he slapped Clarinha's face and ordered her to leave without listening to her story.

Clarinha went at last to the back door of the palace and asked there for work. The queen happened to be in the kitchen with her son, and overheard the young girl's plea. "We do not need anyone," she said, and turned her away. But the prince, impressed by Clarinha's beauty, cried, "Take the girl on, Mother, do. There must be something she can do, if it is only to mind the ducks."

So Clarinha became the duck girl. But again the eagle made trouble for her, causing one or two of the ducks to die each day. Clarinha cried bitterly when the queen scolded her, and the prince suggested she be given some sewing to do instead.

One day, before the prince set out to visit his betrothed far away, he asked the servants of the palace what he could bring them back as gifts. Each one of them made some request of the prince—that is, all except Clarinha. The prince insisted. "Then bring me a stone from the palace, sire," she answered at last.

When the prince arrived in that far-off country, he was told that the princess had disappeared and that the entire population was in mourning. Sadly the prince collected the small gifts for his servants and the stone for Clarinha, and left for his home.

As he entered the palace, the prince suddenly suspected who Clarinha really was. He gave her the stone and quickly went to her chamber and hid himself under the bed to see what she would do with it.

Clarinha entered her room. Locking the door behind her, she placed the stone on a table and addressed it thus: "Stone from the palace of my mother, listen to what has befallen me," and she unburdened herself of everything the eagle had caused to happen. "Open up, stone, with edges sharp as razors, so I can lie on them." No sooner had she finished speaking than the stone split in two pieces with a loud crack.

The prince scrambled out from beneath the bed and took Clarinha in his arms.

"Why did you not tell me this before, beloved?" he asked gently.

"Because you might not have believed me. No one else did. And besides, the eagle told me I must work, and I chose to work while I am young and strong, and not later on when I am old and it is hard. But I was never without hope that you would find me," and Clarinha smiled at her prince.

Soon they were married, and Clarinha returned to her mother and her own land with the prince.

THE LISTENING KING

There was once a king whose passion it was to listen outside people's doors. He was known far and wide, therefore, as the Listening King.

One night he stood listening outside a certain door, and he heard a voice say, "I would like most of all to marry the king's baker, for then I would always have the best and freshest of bread in my larder."

The king heard a second voice say, "That's not for me. I'd marry the king's cook, for then I'd eat the same famous dishes as the king himself."

The king heard a third voice say, "It is the Listening King himself that I would marry."

The king went home to his palace and thought and thought. Next day he ordered the three girls whose voices he had heard to be brought before him.

"You wish to wed my baker?" he asked the first.

"Yes, sire," she answered.

"You wish to wed my cook?" he asked the second.

"Yes, sire," came the reply.

"And you, little one," the king said to the youngest. "You wish to marry me?"

"Yes, my King," was the answer.

The king then ordered the baker and the cook to marry the two oldest girls, and he himself took the youngest for his wife. At first the baker's wife and the cook's wife were very jealous of their sister's good fortune, and thought to plot against her.

But the king ordered them brought before him. "Never forget," he told them, "that I am the Listening King. I know all about your schemes. I will always know. So forget them. Go away and rejoice and get fat in your own good fortune."

THE MONKEY'S POMEGRANATE

There was once a monkey who perched at the top of an olive tree eating a pomegranate. It happened that a seed dropped to the ground beneath the olive tree, and after a short time a pomegranate tree began to grow.

When the monkey saw the pomegranate tree growing, he went to the owner of the olive grove and said to him, "Dig up your olive tree, so that my pomegranate tree may grow."

The man replied, "I won't do it."

Then the monkey went to court and said to the judge, "Make the man dig up his olive tree, so that my pomegranate tree may grow."

"I won't do it," said the judge.

Then the monkey went to the king and said to him, "O

King, take the staff of office from the judge since he won't make the man dig up the olive tree so that my pomegranate tree may grow."

"I won't do it," said the king.

Then the monkey went to the queen, and said to her, "O Queen, make the king angry, since the king won't take the staff of office from the judge, since the judge won't make the man dig up his olive tree so that my pomegranate tree may grow."

"I won't do it," said the queen.

Then the monkey went to a mouse and said to him, "O mouse, go nibble at the ankles of the queen, since the queen won't make the king angry, since the king won't take the staff of office from the judge, since the judge won't make the man dig up his olive tree so that my pomegranate tree may grow."

"I won't do it," said the mouse.

Then the monkey went to a cat and said, "O cat, eat the mouse since the mouse won't nibble at the ankles of the queen, since the queen won't make the king angry, since the king won't take the staff of office from the judge, since the judge won't make the man dig up his olive tree so that my pomegranate tree may grow."

"I won't do it," answered the cat.

Then the monkey went to a dog and said to him, "O dog, bite the cat since the cat won't eat the mouse, since the mouse won't nibble at the ankles of the queen, since the queen won't make the king angry, since the king won't take the staff of office from the judge, since the judge won't make the man dig up his olive tree so that my pomegranate tree may grow."

"I won't do it," said the dog.

Then the monkey went to a stick and said, "O stick, hit the dog since the dog won't bite the cat, since the cat won't eat the mouse, since the mouse won't nibble at the ankles of the queen, since the queen won't make the king angry, since the king won't take the staff of office from the judge, since the judge won't make the man dig up his olive tree so that my pomegranate tree may grow."

"I won't do it," said the stick.

Then the monkey went to a fire and said, "O fire, burn the stick since the stick won't hit the dog, since the dog won't bite the cat, since the cat won't eat the mouse, since the mouse won't nibble at the ankles of the queen, since the queen won't make the king angry, since the king won't take the staff of office from the judge, since the judge won't make the man dig up his olive tree so that my pomegranate tree may grow."

"I won't do it," said the fire.

Then the monkey went to some water and said, "O water, douse the fire since the fire won't burn the stick, since the stick won't hit the dog, since the dog won't bite the cat, since the cat won't eat the mouse, since the mouse won't nibble at the ankles of the queen, since the queen won't make the king angry, since the king won't take the staff of office from the judge, since the judge won't make the man dig up his olive tree so that my pomegranate tree may grow."

"I won't do it," said the water.

Then the monkey went to an ox and said, "O ox, drink the water since the water won't douse the fire, since the fire won't burn the stick, since the stick won't hit the dog, since the dog won't bite the cat, since the cat won't eat the mouse, since the mouse won't nibble at the ankles of the queen, since the queen won't make the king angry, since the king won't take the staff of office from the judge, since the judge won't make the man dig up the olive tree so that my pomegranate tree may grow."

"I won't do it," said the ox.

Then the monkey went to a butcher and said, "O butcher, kill the ox since the ox won't drink the water, since the water won't douse the fire, since the fire won't burn the stick, since the stick won't hit the dog, since the dog won't bite the cat, since the cat won't eat the mouse, since the mouse won't nibble at the ankles of the queen, since the queen won't make the king angry, since the king won't take the staff of office from the judge, since the judge won't make the man dig up his olive tree so that my pomegranate tree may grow."

"I won't do it," said the butcher.

Then the monkey went to Death and said, "O Death, take the butcher since the butcher won't kill the ox, since the ox won't drink the water, since the water won't douse the fire, since the fire won't burn the stick, since the stick won't hit the dog, since the dog won't bite the cat, since the cat won't eat the mouse, since the mouse won't nibble at the ankles of the queen, since the queen won't make the king angry, since the king won't take the staff of office from the judge, since the judge won't make the man dig up his olive tree so that my pomegranate tree may grow."

Death went to take the butcher, but the butcher said to him, "Don't take me, I'll kill the ox."

And the ox said, "Don't kill me, I'll drink the water."

And the water said, "Don't drink me, I'll douse the fire."

And the fire said, "Don't douse me, I'll burn the stick."

And the stick said, "Don't burn me, I'll hit the dog."

And the dog said, "Don't hit me, I'll bite the cat."

And the cat said, "Don't bite me, I'll eat the mouse."

And the mouse said, "Don't eat me, I'll nibble at the ankles of the queen."

And the queen said, "Don't nibble at my ankles, I'll make the king angry."

And the king said, "Don't make me angry, I'll take the staff of office from the judge."

And the judge said, "Don't take away my staff of office, I'll make the man dig up his olive tree."

And the man said, "I'll dig up my olive tree."

And he dug up his olive tree and the monkey watched his pomegranate tree grow.

THE OWL AND THE WOLF

A wolf, walking in the wood, stopped beneath the tall pine where the owl was sitting on her nest.

Looking at him saw against the trunk of the tree with his tail, the owl feared he would cut it down. "O friend wolf," she cried, "don't saw down my pine, or my children will fall out of the nest and be killed."

"If you don't want me to saw the tree, come down," said the wolf.

The owl was unwilling to do this, but she hopped from branch to branch, lower and lower. "What do you want of me?" she asked the wolf.

"I want to give you a message, so come down further," he replied.

"Say it from there, O wolf, my hearing is good," said the owl.

"I won't hurt you, come on down," the wolf requested once again. The owl became careless and hopped to the ground, where the wolf snapped her up.

Inside the wolf's mouth the owl spoke out. "Friend wolf, don't chew me up, for I wish to make a will," she begged.

"What's the need for that?" growled the wolf.

"Then let me say goodbye to my children up in the nest," pleaded the owl.

"If I let you go up there, you'll never come down to me again," was the reply.

"Then at least call up to my children, and say, 'I ate owl,' so they will know I have not left them willingly," said the owl.

Softly, opening his mouth only a crack, the wolf said, "I ate owl."

"O friend wolf, talk louder, or they'll not hear you."

Again the wolf muttered, "I ate owl."

"Louder," said the owl. "They can't possibly hear you."

And the wolf forgot where the owl was and opened his

mouth wide and shouted, "I ate owl."

Immediately the owl flew out and up to the topmost boughs of the tall pine. Safe on her nest once more, she called down to the wolf, "Maybe another owl you'll eat, but not me."

THE COW MAIDEN

There was once a king with three sons. One day he said to them, "My sons, it is time for you to go out into the world. Whichever one of you returns with the most beautiful wife will win my kingdom."

The three princes set out on their journey. In no time at all the oldest of them found and married the beautiful daughter of a baker and the second of them found and married the beautiful daughter of a smith.

The youngest son traveled through many distant lands, but nowhere was he able to find a beautiful girl whom he could love.

One day, after crossing a great open field, he dismounted from his horse and lay down in the shade of a tree to sleep. When he awoke he saw in front of him a tall tower that he had not noticed before. It had no door, only a small window high above the ground. Still tired, the young prince lay still for a while and watched. At last an old woman came in sight. She went to the foot of the tower, knocked on its wall, and said:

> "Arcello, Arcello,
>   Let down your long hair,
>   I wish to climb up
>   Its golden stair."

Amazed, the youngest son saw a thick braid of golden hair roll out of the window, so long that it reached to the ground. He caught his breath at its loveliness. The old woman clasped the braid of hair and climbed up it as though it were a rope, disappearing inside the window. A short while later she came to the window again, climbed down the rope of golden hair, and went away.

The youngest prince, desirous of seeing the owner of such beauty, went to the foot of the tower beneath the window, knocked on the wall, and repeated the words of the old woman:

> "Arcello, Arcello,
>   Let down your long hair,
>   I wish to climb up
>   Its golden stair."

And there in the window staring at him was the most beautiful face in all the world. He began to climb up the rope of hair.

"Oh, sir, go away, go away," the girl said quickly. "My mother may return, and she is so skilled in magic, she could do you great harm."

But the youngest prince would not listen. "I will not leave without you," he told her when he reached the window. "I love you and wish to marry you. Come with me. If you do, I will gain the kingdom of my father. But if you refuse, I shall throw myself from this window to the ground in despair."

So the girl agreed to leave with him. She let down her golden hair and the young man climbed down. Then he held out his arms and caught the girl as she jumped to the ground. Together they fled swiftly on the back of the prince's horse toward his own country.

They had not traveled very far, however, before they heard a voice behind them calling, "Stop, my cruel daughter, stop. Do not leave me here alone in the world."

But the girl only clung more tightly to the young prince as they galloped away.

The old woman called after them again. "At least look

back, my daughter, so that I may give you my blessing," she said.

The girl turned her head and looked back.

"Ah, beautiful face," said the old woman, "for your cruelty toward your mother I shall bewitch you. From this day on, may you have the face of a cow." Immediately the beautiful girl's face turned into that of a cow.

When the prince and his bride arrived at the palace, everyone laughed at the sight of the young girl with the face of a cow. How could the youngest son have married *her*, they asked each other.

The prince described to his brothers what had happened, but they did not believe him. Only the queen was sorry for her youngest son and believed his story. She thought if in some way she could delay the ceremony at which the king was to choose the most beautiful of his sons' brides, perhaps the girl's mother would forgive her daughter and restore her former beauty. So the queen commanded that each of the wives of her three sons must embroider a perfect handkerchief before the ceremony took place.

The wives of the oldest sons, the baker's daughter and the blacksmith's daughter, were both so poorly skilled in embroidery that they planned to deceive the queen and give her delicate handkerchiefs fashioned by someone else. But the poor cow maiden could do nothing but sit and weep. She wept so much that her mother, the old woman, appeared before her.

"You cannot do without me, can you, daughter?" she said. "Now dry your tears and I'll tell you what to do. When the hour comes for you to present your handkerchief to the queen, I will place it in your hand."

On the day that the queen had set, the old woman came to her daughter and gave her a tiny brown nut. The cow maiden took it to the queen, who broke it open. All were amazed to see inside a handkerchief of finest muslin, beautifully embroidered with flowers, ferns, and flying birds.

At last the day came when the wives of the three princes were to be presented to the king, who would choose among them the most beautiful.

Once again the little cow maiden wept and wept, until her mother came. "See, you cannot do without me," she said. "Stop your tears, daughter; I have brought the gown you must wear to appear before the king," and she unfolded a gown embroidered all over in silk and precious gems. When the cow maiden was clothed in this lovely gown, her face looked even more strange, and she wept and wept.

By now everyone at court had assembled before the king. Only she was absent.

"You must go, my daughter," the old woman commanded.

Obediently the girl began to leave her chamber. "Look back," she heard her mother say behind her. She turned her head to look. "You will regain your beauty," pronounced the old woman. "But be sure once again to do as I say in front of the court. While you sit among them, eating at the banquet table, you must fill your sleeves with as many pieces of bacon as you are able, to give to me."

When the cow maiden entered the hall on the arm of the youngest prince, everyone gasped. They no longer saw the strange head of a cow on the body of a young girl, but a lovely face that all agreed was the most beautiful they had ever seen. The spell was lifted.

The king and the entire court sat at the table and began to eat. Throughout the meal the bride of the youngest prince remembered to put little pieces of bacon into the loose sleeves

of her beautiful gown. Thinking this must be some new fashion, the brides of the older princes did the same. When the meal was over, the table was carried away, and the ball commenced.

As the brides danced, little pieces of bacon began to fall from their sleeves, and the dancers slipped and slithered about the floor. The queen was very angry and demanded to know who was responsible for the state of the floor. The wives of the older princes explained how they had done the same as the young girl. All three of the brides shook their sleeves to show the queen, and from two of them fell more pieces of bacon. But from the sleeves of the most beautiful

fell not bacon but pearls, diamonds, and the freshest of flowers. Everyone acclaimed the onetime cow maiden the most beautiful, and the king named his youngest son to be king after him.

The wives of the two older princes were ashamed of themselves for their previous mockery of the cow maiden and for their jealousy of her beauty. And she who was now proclaimed queen as bride of the youngest son also bowed her head in shame. She knew she could never have won the contest without the help of her mother, whom she had left alone so cruelly. "She will live in the palace with us," the young prince told his bride, and they smiled together.

THE COCKROACH AND
THE MOUSE

While sweeping her house one day, a pretty cockroach came upon a cruzado dropped beneath a table. Picking it up, she went to a neighbor for advice.

"O neighbor, what shall I do with the cruzado I found?" she said.

"If I were in your shoes," answered her neighbor, "I would buy sweetmeats or cake with it."

"That sounds greedy to me," thought the cockroach to herself. "I'll see what my other neighbor has to say."

"You're a pretty little bug," said the other neighbor. "If I were in your shoes, I'd buy flowers, ribbons, bracelets of gold, and a pair of earrings, and sit before my open window, singing:

" 'Who'd like to marry me,
     A pretty cockroach, and a good one, too.' "

The pretty cockroach went to buy the flowers, ribbons, bracelets of gold, and a pair of earrings. At home again, she adorned herself with them, and went to sit at her window, singing:

> "Who'd like to marry me,
>   A pretty cockroach, and a good one, too."

An ox passed by the window and said, "I'd like to."

"Let me hear how you speak, ox. Say something more," said the cockroach.

"Moo-oo, moo-oo!" said the ox.

"Oh, what a noise! I cannot marry you, you'd wake the children up at night." And the pretty cockroach began her song again:

> "Who'd like to marry me,
>   A pretty cockroach, and a good one, too."

A gray donkey passed beneath the window and stopped when he heard the song. "I'd like to," he said.

"Let me hear you talk again," said the pretty cockroach.

"Ee-aw, ee-aw," brayed the donkey.

"Oh, what a din! I cannot marry you, for the children surely would be kept awake at night," and the cockroach began her song again.

When a dog came by and stopped to answer her, the cockroach said to him, "Let me hear again how you speak."

And the dog said "Woof, woof" in reply.

"That's far too loud, I'm afraid," said the cockroach. "The children would wake up, I'm sure."

A cat passed beneath the window.

"Let me hear you again," said the pretty cockroach, after the cat said he wished to marry her.

"Meow, meow," said the cat.

"No, no, that won't do at all, you'd wake the children in the night."

Then a little mouse passed under her window. "I'd like to marry you," said the mouse.

"Talk to me some more," said the cockroach.

"Squeak, squeak, squeak," answered the little mouse. "I'd like to marry you."

"That's very lovely," said the cockroach. "I'd like to marry you too."

So the mouse, whose name was *João Ratão*, or Johnny Mouse, married the pretty cockroach and they were very happy.

When Sunday came, the cockroach wished to go to church. "You watch over my pot," she said to Johnny Mouse. "There are beans cooking in it for our dinner."

Johnny Mouse went very close to the fire, and put his hand into the pot to find out if the beans were done. His hand stayed in the pot, so he tried to pull it out with his other hand. But that also stayed in the pot. Then Johnny put one foot in the pot, and could not remove it. He put in the other foot. Little by little, Johnny Mouse fell into the pot and was cooked, together with the beans.

When the pretty little cockroach returned from church, she could not see Johnny Mouse, though she searched everywhere. "Oh well, he'll turn up when he wishes," she said to herself. "I'll have a helping of beans while I'm waiting for him." But when she dished up the beans, she saw poor Johnny Mouse lying cooked on her plate. She began to weep and wail.

"Whatever's the matter, my pretty little cockroach? And why do you cry so hard?" asked the three-legged stool by the window.

"Johnny Mouse is dead, that's why I'm crying," sobbed the cockroach.

"Then I'll whirl around and around and around," said the three-legged stool by the window.

"Whatever's the matter, O three-legged stool? Why do you whirl around and around?" asked the door to the street.

"Johnny Mouse is dead and our pretty cockroach is crying. That's why I whirl around and around," answered the three-legged stool.

"Then I'll open and close with a bang," said the door to the street.

"Whatever's the matter, O door to the street? Why do you open and close with a bang?" asked a rafter high in the ceiling.

"Johnny Mouse is dead, our pretty cockroach is crying, the three-legged stool is whirling around and around, that's why I open and close with a bang," answered the door to the street.

"Then I'll break myself in two," said the rafter high in the ceiling.

"Whatever's the matter, O rafter high in the ceiling? Why do you break yourself in two?" asked a pine tree outside the door.

"Johnny Mouse is dead, our pretty cockroach is crying, the three-legged stool is whirling around and around, the door to the street is opening and closing with a bang, that's why I break myself in two," answered the rafter high in the ceiling.

"Then I'll uproot myself," said the pine tree outside the door.

"Whatever's the matter, O pine tree outside the door?" said the birds resting in its branches. "Why are you uprooting yourself?"

"Johnny Mouse is dead, our pretty cockroach is crying, the three-legged stool is whirling around and around, the door to the street is opening and closing with a bang, the rafter high in the ceiling is breaking itself in two, that's why I'm uprooting myself," answered the pine tree outside the door.

"Then we'll cry out our eyes," said the birds resting in the pine branches. And they flew to the fountain of precious water nearby to drink.

"Whatever's the matter, little birds?" asked the fountain of precious water. "Why do you cry out your eyes?"

"Johnny Mouse is dead, our pretty cockroach is crying, the three-legged stool is whirling around and around, the door to the street is opening and closing with a bang, the rafter high in the ceiling is breaking itself in two, the pine tree outside the door is uprooting itself, that's why we cry out our eyes," said the little birds.

"Then I'll dry up my precious water," said the fountain.

The children of the king came to the fountain, to fill their pitchers with precious water.

"Whatever's the matter, O fountain, that you've dried up your precious water?" asked the king's children.

"Johnny Mouse is dead, our pretty cockroach is crying, the three-legged stool is whirling around and around, the door to the street is opening and closing with a bang, the rafter high in the ceiling is breaking itself in two, the pine tree outside the door is uprooting itself, the birds resting in its branches are crying out their eyes, that's why I dried up my precious water," answered the fountain.

"Then we will break our pitchers," said the king's children, and returned to the palace.

"Whatever's the matter, children, and why did you break your pitchers?" asked the queen of the wonderful skirts.

"Johnny Mouse is dead, our pretty cockroach is crying, the three-legged stool is whirling around and around, the door to the street is opening and closing with a bang, the

rafter high in the ceiling is breaking itself in two, the pine
tree outside the door is uprooting itself, the little birds in its
branches are crying out their eyes, the fountain is drying up
its precious water, that's why we are breaking our pitchers,"
said the children of the king.

"Then I'll go into our kitchen, children dear," said the
queen of the wonderful skirts, "and I'll find you another
mouse, to give to the pretty cockroach to marry." But the
queen couldn't find any mouse in her kitchen.

"Whatever's the matter, my queen of the wonderful
skirts?" asked the king. "Why do you go searching in the
kitchen?"

"Johnny Mouse is dead, our pretty cockroach is crying,
the three-legged stool is whirling around and around, the door
to the street is opening and closing with a bang, the rafter

high in the ceiling is breaking itself in two, the pine tree outside the door is uprooting itself, the birds resting in its branches are crying out their eyes, the fountain is drying up its precious water, your children have broken their pitchers, and I cannot find another mouse in the kitchen for the pretty cockroach to wed," answered the queen.

"Then I'll go to the stables," said the king. "I'm sure to find a little mouse for the pretty cockroach to marry." And he did.

ABOUT THE AUTHOR

Patricia Tracy Lowe grew up in Oxford, England, where her father was a famous classical scholar. She was educated in England, France, Italy, and the United States and has since traveled in many countries. She is now a freelance editor, writer and translator, living in New York City. She is married, with three grown-up sons.

ABOUT THE ARTIST

Anne Marie Jauss was born in Germany and studied art in Munich. She left Germany in 1932, and for the next fourteen years she lived in Portugal, where she became deeply interested in Portuguese history and folklore. It was she who selected and translated the stories in this book.

Since 1946 Miss Jauss has lived in the United States. She has had several one-man shows and has illustrated over fifty books, among them several written by herself.